Happy Birthday Baby Bop!

PUFFIN BOOKS

Dear Parents

This book follows Baby Bop™ on her third birthday. A birthday celebration is one of the most important days of the year for young children. They enjoy the increased attention, the feeling of "being big", and, of course, the anticipation of a party with friends, cake and presents! Young children will easily identify with Baby Bop's excitement on her special day.

We consider books to be lifelong gifts that develop and enhance the love of reading. We hope you enjoy reading along with Baby Bop!

Mary Ann Dudko, Ph.D.
Margie Larsen, M.Ed.
Early Childhood Educational Specialists

Art Director: Tricia Legault
Designer: Jo Carol Arnold

PUFFIN BOOKS

Published by the Penguin Group under licence from Lyons Partnership, L.P.
Penguin Books Ltd, 27 Wrights Lane, London W8 5TZ, England
Penguin Books USA Inc., 375 Hudson Street, New York, New York 10014, USA
Penguin Books Australia Ltd, Ringwood, Victoria, Australia
Penguin Books Canada Ltd, 10 Alcorn Avenue, Toronto, Ontario, Canada M4V 3B2
Penguin Books (NZ) Ltd, 182–190 Wairau Road, Auckland 10, New Zealand

Penguin Books Ltd, Registered Offices: Harmondsworth, Middlesex, England

First published in the USA by Barney Publishing 1995
Published in Puffin Books 1996
10 9 8 7 6 5 4 3 2 1

Made and printed in Italy by Printers srl – Trento

Happy Birthday Baby Bop!

Written by Linda Cress Dowdy
Photography by Dennis Full

Today is my birthday!
I'm going to be 3.
It's such a fun number.
Please count with me—1-2-3.

There's a party for 3.
We'll have fun and games!
My best friends are here.
Do you know their names?

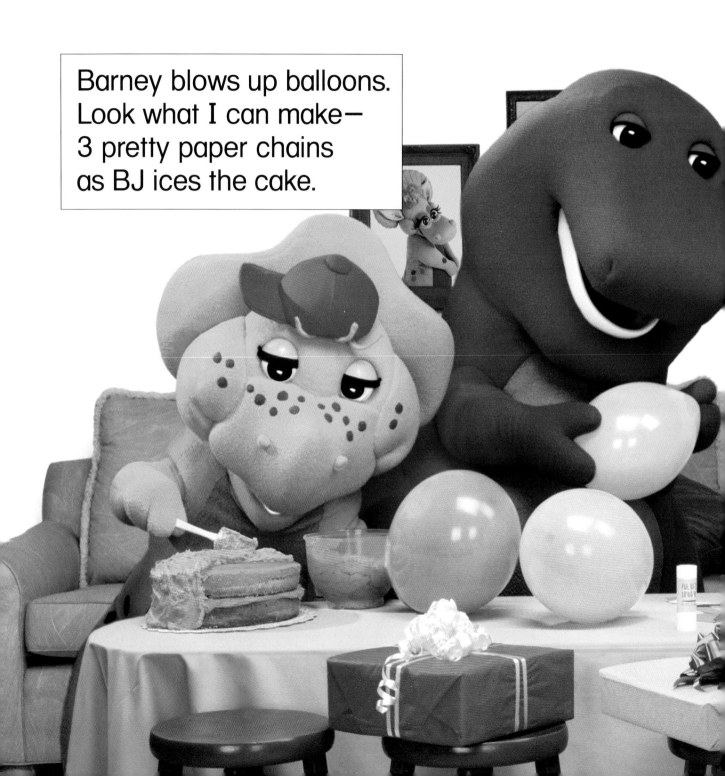

Barney blows up balloons.
Look what I can make—
3 pretty paper chains
as BJ ices the cake.

Pin the tail on the donkey
is a fun game to play.
Spin around 3 times.
Walk quickly this way.

I count 3 presents,
each wrapped with a bow.
What can they be?
I can't wait to know!

What a wonderful gift.
A tricycle for me!
It has 3 wheels.
Count them and see!

Let's sing "Happy Birthday".
It's my favourite song.
We'll sing it together.
Come on, sing along!

1-2-3 candles
on my birthday cake!
I will blow them all out.
What wish should I make?

What a fun birthday party
for my friends and me.
I'm a big girl now.
Look at me! I am 3!